P9-DGE-271
What
Are
You
Glad
About?
What
Are
You
Mad
About?
This book
belongs to:

ALSO BY JUDITH VIORST

Alexander and the Terrible, Horrible, No Good, Very Bad Day

Alexander, Who's Not (Do You Hear Me? I Mean It!) Going to Move

Alexander, Who's Trying His Best to Be the Best Boy Ever

Alexander, Who Used to Be Rich Last Sunday

Earrings!

The Good-Bye Book

If I Were in Charge of the World and Other Worries: Poems for Children and Their Parents

Just in Case

Lulu and the Brontosaurus

Lulu Walks the Dogs

Lulu's Mysterious Mission

My Mama Says There Aren't Any Zombies, Ghosts, Vampires, Creatures, Demons, Monsters, Fiends, Goblins, or Things

Rosie and Michael

Sad Underwear and Other Complications: More Poems for Children and Their Parents

Super-Completely and Totally the Messiest!

The Tenth Good Thing About Barney

What Are You Glad About? What Are You Mad About?

Poems
for
When a Person
Needs a Poem

Judith Viorst
with art by Lee White

A Caitlyn Dlouhy Book
Atheneum Books for Young Readers
New York London Toronto Sydney New Delhi

CONSULTANTS

Sophie Pitofsky Mode, Chief Consultant
Henry Pitofsky Mode
Leo [Oberdorfer] Nyberg
Sasha Azizi Rosenfeld
Benjamin Carlo Gwadz Viorst
Nathaniel Redding Gwadz Viorst
Isaac Rigel Viorst
Olivia Rigel Viorst
Toby Rigel Viorst

atheneum

ATHENEUM BOOKS FOR YOUNG READERS
An imprint of Simon & Schuster Children's Publishing Division
1230 Avenue of the Americas, New York, New York 10020

Also available in an Atheneum Books for Young Readers hardcover edition
Book design by Ann Bobco
The text for this book was set in Aged.
The illustrations for this book were rendered digitally.
Manufactured in China
1116 SCP
First Atheneum Books for Young Readers paperback edition February 2017
10 9 8 7 6 5 4 3 2 1
The Library of Congress has cataloged the hardcover edition as follows:
Names: Viorst, Judith, author. | White, Lee, 1970- illustrator.
Title: What are you glad about? what are you mad about? : poems for when a person needs a poem / Judith Viorst ; illustrated by Lee White.
Description: First edition. | New York : Atheneum Books for Young Readers, [2015]
Identifiers: LCCN 2015027236 | ISBN 978-1-4814-2355-7 (hc) | ISBN 978-1-4814-2356-4 (pbk) | ISBN 978-1-4814-2357-1 (eBook)
Subjects: LCSH: Emotions–Juvenile poetry.
Classification: LCC PS3572.I6 A6 2015b | DDC 811/.54–dc23
LC record available at http://lccn.loc.gov/2015027236

In loving memory of
Elaine Konigsburg,
the first to listen to these poems
–J. V.

For my silly little munchkin, Emerson
–L.W.

CONTENTS

Help

The Best and the Worst

Songs of the Seasons

Mysteries

Not Done Yet

Index

HOW
ARE
YOU
FEELING
TODAY?

What Are You Glad About? What Are You Mad About?

If you had just one color to paint the whole world,
Would it be orange or gray?
If you had just one message to give to the world,
Would it be grrr or hooray?
If you had just one place you could live in this world,
Would you choose here or away?
What are you glad about?
What are you mad about?
How are you feeling today?

Did you wake up this morning all smiley inside?
Does life taste like ice cream and cake?
Or does it seem more like your goldfish just died
And your insides are one great big ache?
Do you wish you could go in a closet and hide?
Or would you rather go play?
What are you glad about?
Mad about? Sad about?
How are you feeling today?

When they ask you to do something, will you say yes?
Or will your answer be no?
Do you think that you get what you want—or much less?
Are you shrinking or starting to grow?
Is that person you see in the mirror a mess?
Or is that person okay?
What are you glad about?
Mad, sad, or bad about?
How are you feeling today?

All Alone Inside My Very Own Skin

I'm all alone inside my very own skin.
That's how it is, and how it's always been.
We are each a one-and-only
But at times I feel so lonely
That I wish I could invite somebody in.

I'm all alone here—I, myself, and me.
That's just one person, though it sounds like three.
If you've nothing else to do,
And if you're feeling lonely too,
Perhaps you'd like to keep me company.

Such a Lovely Girl

The moms, they all love Anna May.
She's such a lovely girl, they say.
There's no one sweeter, kinder, or politer.
I really hate to hear them say
You must be more like Anna May
When I don't want to be—I want to bite—her.

She's such a lovely girl, they swear.
She gets good grades. She's got great hair.
She tries to be the best, and who can stop her?
She likes to help. She likes to share.
She always wears clean underwear.
She's practically a saint—I'd like to bop her.

Each night I go to bed and pray
That Anna May will move away
To someplace far—perhaps the Isle of Man. It
Could be New Zealand, Paraguay,
Nepal, the Gobi Desert. Hey,
It even—yay!—could be a whole new planet.

I'm sick of having her adored
By all the moms, while I'm ignored.
She's such a lovely girl, they always tell us.
She's ten, I'm zero on the board
Of any game that's being scored.
What possibly could make you think I'm jealous?

Much More Than Terrified

I know there's a monster lurking inside
My closet. I am terrified.
I can hear his breathing—
Fierce and fast and furious.
But I've never met a monster before,
So I'm going to open my closet door
Because, much more than terrified,
I am curious.

Sorry?

I did it! I did it! I did it!
Although all the grown-ups forbid it.
I knew right away that it wasn't okay,
But even good children can't always obey.
And yesterday morning I couldn't obey,
So I did it.

I did it! I did it! I did it!
I did what I shouldn't, then hid it.
I wanted to blame it on three other guys
Except I turn red when I start telling lies.
And everyone knows, when I start telling lies,
That I did it.

I did it! I did it! I did it!
And now I will have to admit it.
I'll say that I'm sorry for what I have done.
I'll say lots of sorries. I won't mention fun,
Although I had fun, lots of fun, SO MUCH FUN,
When I did it.

The Sillies

I feel like wearing mismatched socks,
One purple and one orange.
I'd like to wear them on my ears,
Or maybe on my borange.
You wonder what a borange is?
Go ask my cousin Bill. He's
The guy who knows the answers since
I went and caught the sillies.

I feel like eating lamps for lunch,
And then some rugs for supper.
And for dessert I'd like to try
A kerwait or a gupper.
You don't get what I'm saying? You
Must check with cousin Gil. He's
The guy who knows what's doing since
I went and caught the sillies.

I feel like flying to Veezu
On my next school vacation,
Unless I go to Cloop instead.
You want an explanation
Of where these places are? You'd best
Call up my cousin Phil. He's
The guy who knows what's flying since
I went and caught the sillies.

Get serious, my mama says.
She thinks that I'm outrageous.
And also a bad influence.
Perhaps even contagious.
She tells me stop my nonsense now–
It's giving her the willies,
But I'm not stopping till you all
Have gone and caught the sillies.

SCHOOL

SCHOOL STUFF

What I've Learned at School

John F. Kennedy was our thirty-fifth president.
Earth is a planet revolving around the sun.
Not everyone's mom puts an I-love-you note in their lunch
box next to their lunch.
And not everyone remembers to flush when they're done.

Every mammal has hair, and a whale is a mammal.
A poem is a poem even if it doesn't rhyme.
Teachers don't like to hear stories about how the wind blew
your homework away.
And the school bus won't wait if you aren't there on time.

Annapolis is the capital of Maryland.
And twenty-one divided by seven is three.
And wearing a black leather jacket won't make you the
coolest kid in the class
As long as your favorite movie is still *E.T.*

Alexander Graham Bell invented the telephone.
You've got to stop talking once the exam begins.
You're never supposed to make fun of the other team
when it loses a game.
And you're never ever supposed to cry when it wins.

Mix red and yellow together if you want orange.
If you want green, you need to mix yellow and blue.
I also have learned the difference between metamorphic
and igneous rocks,
And between boys and girls, but I'm not telling you.

School Lunch

There was trouble this afternoon at the school cafeteria.
Somebody sat on Mary's PB&J.
The girl went into a state of total hysteria
And poured ketchup all over the sandwich-sitter's tray,
Who then took his burger and plopped it on top of Mary
'S head, after dipping it first in the ketchup-ed tray,
Which is why she is eating a burger that's slurpy and hairy,
And why he is eating a smelly PB&J.

Reading and Writing

To learn the English language, rules are needed,
So many rules my head will soon explode.
The dog I FEED, I've FED—I can't say FEEDED.
The candles I BLOW out, I BLEW, not BLOWED.

If I should CHEAT—I never would—I CHEATED.
If I should CRY—I sometimes do—I CRIED.
But when I EAT a snack, I haven't EATED.
And when I BUY, I cannot say I BUYED.

I READ a book. That doesn't mean I READED,
Though if I BOSS you, I can say I BOSSED.
They're making me say LED instead of LEADED.
And if I LOSE, I haven't LOSED, I've LOST.

The lambs who BLEAT are always lambs who BLEATED.
But moms who DRIVE are always moms who DROVE.
I'm positive that when I WEED, I WEEDED.
But when I DIVE, have I just DIVED or DOVE?

I know BLED goes with BLEED. It isn't BLEEDED.
CHOSE goes with CHOOSE, but SQUOZE won't go
with SQUEEZE.
These rules have left me BEATEN though not BEATED.
I think I'd rather try to learn Chinese.

Arithmetrick

The Lesson

Pick a number.
Shh, don't tell.
Add 6.
Add 5.
Add 9.

Take 2 away.
Take 4 away.
Add 8.
You're doing fine.

Now take away
The number that
You started with,
And then

Divide by 2.
Take 1 away.
I bet
You're left with
10.

The Homework

How did I do that?
Figure it out.
Then ask a friend to pick
A number (shh). Now you can play
Your own arithmetrick.

Daniel Tries Out for the School Play

I thought they would choose me for star of the show.
I learned all the lines that I needed to know.
I sang the songs loudly and sang them in tune.
But then, after watching us all afternoon,
They picked Jackson.

Okay, so I tried out for Jackson's best friend.
There's a really cool dance that he does at the end.
And nobody knew the steps better than I.
But then, after six other kids got to try,
They picked Carlos.

Well, maybe the bad dude is who I should play.
He sneers and he snarls and has plenty to say.
So I sneered and I snarled and I showed them
my stuff.
But then, when they thanked me and said,
"That's enough,"
They picked Tyler.

Some kids might start feeling discouraged, I guess.
There's one big part left, but it's not mine unless
I agree to wear lipstick and dress in a dress.

I said yes.

This Substitute Teacher Is Really into Rhyming

Icicle, bicycle,
Holiest, lowliest,
Kalamazoo and achoo.
Spaghetti and steady
And also confetti . . .
Rhyming is such fun to do!

Gentle and lentil
And coincidental.
Gorilla, a pill a day too.
Busy and dizzy
And what about is he?
Rhyming is such fun to do!

Now we could get weirder
And rhyme it with theater,
Then dare to do matzah and lotsa,
As in lotsa luck.
But I'll bet you a buck
That nobody comes up with plotz, a
Word that means faint or collapse from surprise,
Which maybe just happened to you,
Though I hope you've had time
To discover that rhym-
Ing is such fun, so much fun to do.

Much more fun than eating a shoe.
Or spilling a bowl of beef stew.
Or weeping and wailing boo-hoo.
Or being all covered with glue.
Or sharing a bed with a gnu.
Or smelling a smell that's pee-U.
Or—

Uh-oh!—it's 10:52.
Class over. Bye-bye. Toodle-oo.

ABOUT THE FAMILY

My Papa

My papa is my daddy's dad.
He tickles and he teases.
He makes me sandwiches for lunch.
The best are his grilled cheeses.

My papa helps remind me of
My thank-yous and my pleases.
But I don't need reminders when
I'm eating his grilled cheeses.

My papa rides a bicycle,
And even skis on skises.
But what he's really champion of
Is grilling his grilled cheeses.

My papa snores ferocious snores
And sneezes mighty sneezes.
But nothing shakes and nothing breaks
When he makes his grilled cheeses.

My papa doesn't hear too well.
He's achy in the kneeses.
But he's completely perfect when
He's grilling his grilled cheeses.

My papa's traveled everywhere.
He's sailed the seven seases.
But I think he likes staying home
To make me his grilled cheeses.

When I get to be president,
I'll banish prunes and peases,
And name my papa head of the
Department of Grilled Cheeses.

Why Cats Are Better Than My Older Sister

They never tell you what to do.
They never ever yell at you.
They don't think that they're always right.
They're prettier to look at, too.

They do not mind a messy room.
They aren't stinky with perfume.
And when they fight, they friendly fight—
More like a pat than a kaboom.

They don't act like a year-round Grinch.
They don't, when no one's looking, pinch,
Or chase you from their bed at night,
Or say you haven't grown an inch.

They do not always think they're queen.
They wouldn't be, on purpose, mean,
Or want you out—out!—of their sight.
And though they're clean, they're not *too* clean.

I'd never want to tell them "Scat!"
I've got a secret wish. It's that
Someday, someway, somehow I might
Exchange my sister for a cat.

What I Want to Know About My Dad

My dad comes home
From work, hangs up
His jacket, checks his mail,
Takes out a bowl, and opens up a can.
He's eating all alone tonight.
Here's what I want to know:
Is he a happy, or a lonely, man?

The rest of us
Have gone away.
We're driving to Montclair
To pay a little visit to mom's mom.
My dad's left in this empty house.
Here's what I want to know:
Does he enjoy, or does he hate, the calm?

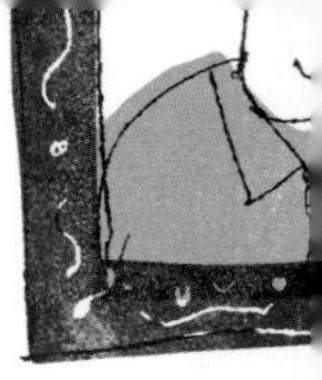

My dad goes up
The stairs, clicks on
The clicker for TV,
Takes off his clothes, and flops upon the bed.
He's sleeping in it by himself.
Here's what I want to know:
Does he wish all of us were there instead?

The house is dark
And locked up tight.
My dad is snoring now,
And having dreams—but pleasant dreams or grim?
He's always watching over us.
Here's what I want to know:
Is anybody watching over him?

Bossy Mom

I can't ride my bike to the far side of town.
My mom says I'm bound to get lost.
There are places she won't let me walk to because
Of the dangerous streets to be crossed.
She treats me as if I am still in first grade
And expects all the rules she has made are obeyed.
(Though there's ten million rules that, I swear, she has made.)
I'm so bossed!

I can't go to bed till I've washed and I've brushed,
And she even makes sure that I've flossed.
And whatever I've worn I'm supposed to pick up
And not leave on the floor where it's tossed.
No matter how long and how loud I complain—
That she's ruining my life! That she's causing me pain!
That she's going to drive me completely insane!—
I get bossed!

In winter I have to wear Eskimo clothes
So I don't catch a chill from the frost.
And she tells me I can't have my ears pierced, although
I could save up and pay what it cost.
She promises someday when I'm finally grown
I will get to be boss and make rules of my own.
But meanwhile I can't even stay home alone.
I'm still bossed!
I'm still getting bossed!
I am so bossed!

New Brother

How come they ever
Thought that I
Would want to have
A brother?
I have a gerbil,
Two nice fish,
A father,
And a mother.
And all the toys
Belonged to me.
And so did
All the kisses.
So just in case
They're wondering,
I want to say that
This is
TURNING OUT TO BE
A BAD IDEA.

TO
MARS

My Grandma

Some grandmas sew your buttons on.
Some bake you oatmeal cookies.
Some have gray hair. My grandma dyes hers red.
Kids' movies leave her snoring,
And she finds all board games boring,
And she's not someone you'd ask to pull your sled.

Some grandmas come to swimming meets
And clap at your recitals
And go with you to playgrounds. Mine won't play.
She'd rather take karate
Than a grandchild to a potty.
And a trip to Disney Land? Uh-uh! No way!

Some grandmas live in houses and
Some grandmas live in condos.
Some grandmas live with grandpas. Mine does not.
She's got a boyfriend—Jerry.
And she says to call him Jerry.
And she hangs out with this Jerry a whole lot.

Some grandmas teach you lessons and
Some make you tasty dinners.
Mine orders in. It's best she doesn't cook.
She'll never knit a sweater.
But I love her much, much better
Than any grandma in a storybook.

More About My Papa

My papa's name is Milton, and
When he was just a kid,
He asked his friends to call him Ace,
But no one ever did.

The other kids had nicknames, and
He thought Ace sounded cool.
But he kept being Milton
Everywhere he went to school.

Just call me Ace, he told the kids
On playgrounds and in parks.
But even though their names were Duke
And Doobie, Rex and Sparks,

They wouldn't call him Ace. He tried
Till he was way past ten,
And understood they never would,
And never tried again.

My papa's kind of old now. He's
Got wrinkles on his face.
And I'm thinking that tomorrow
I will start to call him Ace.

HOME AND AWAY

Places I'd Like, If . . .
or
I Guess Some People Worry More Than Others

I like to wear almost no clothes.
I like the sand between my toes,
The ocean's whisper and its roar,
The sea glass gleaming on the shore.
I like the sun hot on my back.
If killer sharks did not attack,
I'd like beaches.

I like the close-together trees,
The piney smell upon the breeze,
The crunch beneath my hiking shoes,
The birds exchanging daily news,
How soft a rainy woodland feels.
If bears did not eat kids for meals,
I'd like forests.

I like the view from way up high,
The so-near-you-can-touch-it sky,
The tininess of what's below,
The peaks dressed up in caps of snow.
I like the silences, and if
No blizzards blew folks off a cliff,
I'd like mountains.

Some lakes are million-mile-deep lakes.
And prairies have those rattlesnakes.
The water in the desert? None!
The tigers in the jungle? Run!
So many wondrous things to see,
And if I were a different me,
I'd like them.

And We Call It Home

Home is where the you that's truly you lives.
It's where the music of your heart is played.
Home is where you go and what you know gives
You shelter when you're lonely or afraid.
And when the skies turn dark and bad times chase you,
And all the gates are locked and shades are drawn,
There's a place where someone will embrace you,
And keep you safe until a kinder dawn.
And we call it home.

Home is where your dreams have their beginning.
Home is where love's language is first learned.
It's where you needn't worry about winning.
It's where what you receive need not be earned.
And when in anger hurtful words are spoken,
And when you trip and fall into disgrace,
This is where there's help to mend what's broken.
This is what remains your sacred space.
And we call it home.

Home's the hearth from which you're free to travel
Farther than the farthest winds have blown.
Home's the healing place when things unravel,
Where supper's waiting and your name is known.
And when you want to tell your tales of glory,
And speak of what you've done and where you've been,

This is where they'll listen to your story.
This is where they'll always take you in.
And we call it home.
And we call it home.
And we call it home.

Far Away

When I don't like how things are here,
I dream of Far Away,
A place where every day would be
A how-I-like-it day.

No brothers making fun of me.
No teachers saying what
Is eighty-four times seventeen?
No falling on my butt.

No, no you cannot have a dog
Or seconds on that cake.
No blaming me for breaking stuff
I didn't know would break.

No never being chosen first.
No toothaches. No time-outs.
No being told no ice cream till
I eat those Brussels sprouts.

Good-bye, friends, family, everyone.
I'm going up to pack.
But if I miss how things are here,
Will you let me come back?

FRIENDS AND
OTHER PEOPLE

I'm Not My Best Friend's Best Friend Anymore

I'm not my best friend's best friend anymore.
She says I'm Number Three, or maybe Four.
We used to be a Velcro-ed superglued-together *us*.
But now she wants to sit with other kids on the school bus.
We've never had an argument, or even a small fuss,
But I'm not my best friend's best friend anymore.

There wasn't anything we didn't share.
We even wore each other's underwear.
We both loved purple, soccer, Harry Potter, shrimp, and snow.
When I went to the bathroom, she would always need to go.
We once played twenty-seven games of Bingo in a row.
But I'm not my best friend's best friend anymore.

I told her that I didn't care. I lied.
The day we broke up I came home and cried.
My mom says pretty soon I'll find myself a new best friend.
But I just want the old one back. Why did it have to end?
I'm hoping if I put this poem on e-mail and click send
I'll make things be the way they were before
I was not my best friend's best friend anymore.

What Terry Told Me While We Were Eating Our Ice Cream

So this is the kind of kid I'm:
I don't have a dollar or dime.
While others are trying
To save, I keep buying.
I'll start saving some other time.

Whatever I'm given or lent
Is instantly, totally spent.
It slips through my fingers.
Not one penny lingers.
(I'm glad Mom and Dad don't charge rent.)

When I walk a puppy at dawn,
Or babysit, mow someone's lawn,
My pockets start burning
With what I am earning,
And next thing I know it's all gone.

I wish I was making a joke,
But these are true words I just spoke.
This ice cream I'm eating?
I hope you are treating,
Because I am—once again!—broke.

What to Do with a Bully

You could punch him in the nose,
You could stomp him on his toes,
You could give him a fat lip,
Stick your foot out—make him trip,
Jab your elbow in his gut,
Squish his fingers, kick his butt,
Soak him with a water gun,
Twist his arm, or . . .
You could run.

Keeping Up with My Friends

When Charlotte learned to tie her shoes,
I started tying mine.
When Kyle learned cursive, that same day
I cursived every line.
When Tess recited capitals,
I memorized each one.
I wished to show that I could do
Whatever they had done.

When Grace began to take guitar,
I took guitar as well.
And since Zach won that spelling bee,
There's nothing I can't spell.
Nicole is on the swimming team,
So I swim laps galore,
To prove it's true that I can do
What they can do—and more.

Since Maya got a telescope,
I've learned the names of stars.
Now Adam does gymnastics, so
I'm swinging from the bars.
Jill bakes a pie. I bake a pie.
This contest never ends.
Who knew there was so much to do
To keep up with my friends?

Crowded

This chair is a one-person chair
And I am the person who's there.
So remove—now!—your tush
Or I'll give you a push
That will make you fly—*whoosh!*—through the air.

This chair is for one—and no more.
Too bad you were not here before.
But since I was the first
You can cry till you burst
And I'll still make you sit on the floor.

This chair just holds one—and that's it.
Here's NOT where you're going to sit.
Did you say "pretty please"?
Well then, let us both squeeze.
Hmm, it's crowded, but two
people fit.

The Story of Me and Fred

Each time I leave my lunch behind,
He gives me half of his,
Because that is the special kind
Of friend my friend Fred is.

And even though our whole class knows
That soccer is my worst,
Whenever teams are being chose
Fred makes them choose me first.

And if I'm acting like a fool,
Which now and then I might,
Fred doesn't mind. He just stays cool
Until I'm acting right.

And also, when I play guitar
Completely out of tune,
Fred says that though I'm not a star
He thinks I will be soon.

No kid would dare to pick on me.
No bad guy would attack,
For the entire world can see
That Fred has got my back.

So here's the deal I made with Fred:
I get to be his friend
And, in exchange, when I am dead,
He gets my toys. The end.

ABOUT
THIS AND THAT

About This Snake

Silky
Slinky
Slithery
This snake came by to visit me,
And now he's acting like he wants to play.
I do not want to play with snakes.
They give me chills. They give me shakes.
I'm saying "Go!," but he won't go away.

Slowly
Smoothly
Silently
This snake, I think, just smiled at me.
(It's hard to tell his front end from his rear.)
His chin's now resting on my foot.
He's definitely staying put,
Though definitely I don't want him here.

Sleekly
Slickly
Ssssingly
This snake, instead of hissing me,
Blows kisses at me, sighs a gentle sigh.
It's difficult to give a shove
To someone who is so in love.
That's why we're new best friends—this snake and I.

About Time

What a bummer!
What a bummer!
It's a century till summer,
Which, when it arrives, will last
Just half a week before it's past.
Honestly, it makes me sick
That everything that's fun goes quick,
While if you're in a dentist's chair,
It's months till you get out of there.
A bad day's bad for years and years.
A good day starts, then disappears
Much faster than the speed of light.
I'm telling you this isn't right!

It's time that time got redesigned
With pause, fast-forward, and rewind.

25¢
ICE
CRE

About What?

Some people, when they take a trip,
Go straight from here to there,
While others like to travel roundabout:
A zigzag up. A zigzag down.
A zigzag everywhere.
They're always looking for a whole new route.

The zigzaggers will usually
Wear jeans and tennis shoes.
The non-zigzaggers mostly wear a suit,
And mostly call a route a "raut,"
While those in jeans refuse
To call it anything except a "root."

I know which group is wearing suits,
And which is wearing jeans.
I know which group says "root" and which says "raut."
But I've forgotten totally
What any of this means.
Can someone tell me what this poem's about?

This WAY

Just About Ready

I'm ready! I'm ready! I'm just about ready.
I'm just about ready to go.
I'm wearing my jacket, my hat, and my gloves
And my snow boots in case there is snow.
There's lunch in my backpack, along with my homework.
My big science project is done,
And I'll carry it carefully to the school bus,
And I'll—WHAT? Did you just say it's Sun-
day?

HELP

Bubble Gum

I blew a big bubble of bubble gum,
Though my mom and my dad said to stop it.
I blew and I blew and it grew and it grew,
But I kept refusing to pop it.

I blew a big bubble of bubble gum,
And I now am in serious trouble.
For out there, real mad, stand my mom and my dad,
While I am—help!—inside this bubble.

Request

Got a cough and got a sneeze.
Got this aching in my head.
Feeling wobbly in my knees.
Mom says I must stay in bed.

Pain in belly. Rash on neck.
And my throat is super-sore.
I've become a total wreck.
And there's more! There's so much more!

Heart is going *pound-pound-pound.*
Nose is stuffed with something yuck.
In my ears a buzzing sound.
On my chest a ten-ton truck.

I've got sweats and I've got chills.
And my temperature is high.
Tell the doctor no more pills.
If I am about to die,
I WANT CHOCOLATE!

Whoops!

I tell you I am tall enough!
Don't need your help to get that stuff!
I know that you're just trying to be kind.
But I can reach it. Can! And will!
And nothing's gonna break or spill.
No, nothing's gonna—
Whoops! I've changed my mind.

Star Guide

Climb up on the tallest tree
When the sunset fades to black.
Stretch and catch a star for me.
Say I needn't give it back.

With so many shining there
Now that day is finally done,
Certainly the sky can spare
One small unimportant one.

I will hold it in my heart,
Carefully, so it won't break.
I will bring it when I start
On the journey I must take,

On a journey far and long,
Miles and years from all I know
And the places I belong.
Going 'cause it's time to go.

People call this childhood's end.
Wish that I could stay some more,
But instead I must pretend
I'm ready to walk out the door.

And when I feel lost inside,
Too confused to cry or pray,
This small star will be my guide,
Helping me to find my way.

Help Me!

Help me with my homework.
Help me lift this heavy box.
Help me find my sneakers
And some not-too-slimy socks.
Help me chase this dragon
Out from underneath my bed.
Help me fix this headache,
Which is aching my whole head.
Help me wipe the juice up
That I just knocked off the shelf.
Help me walk my dog, which
I'm too tired to walk myself.
Help me please with all my
Ninety-seven other chores.
Then help me make excuses
When you ask for help with yours.

THE BEST AND THE WORST

My Least Favorite Things

Bellyaches, earaches, and teeth that need drilling.
Putting on dress-up shoes—ugly and killing.
Jellyfish, bees, and whatever else stings.
These are among my least favorite things.

Flat tires, vampires, getting all muddy.
Tests for which I have forgotten to study.
Wakened each day by my clock's ding-a-lings.
These are among my least favorite things.

When my tongue's bit,
When my toe's stubbed,
When I need a nurse,
I simply recall my least favorite things,
And then I feel even worse.

No more hot water while taking a shower.
Being expected to eat cauliflower.
Picked to paint scenery, not to play kings.
These are among my least favorite things.

Having to share when I don't feel like sharing.
Wearing a coat it's too hot to be wearing.
Singing the song wrong when everyone sings.
These are among my least favorite things.

When my Coke spills,
When my nose bleeds,
When I'm last, not first,
I simply recall my least favorite things,
And then what's worse becomes worst.

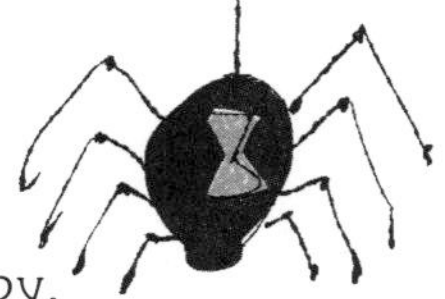

Scorpions, spiders, and all creatures creepy.
Going to bed when I'm not one bit sleepy.
Trying to end this darn poem with an "ings."
These are among my least favorite things.

The Best and the Worst

The best mom? That's my mother.
The best dad? Mine, of course.
The worst thing that could happen?
They're getting a divorce.

I cried until my eyes drowned.
I begged till I was hoarse.
It did not make a difference.
They're getting a divorce.

The best news? They still love me,
And always will, of course.
The worst news? That won't stop them
From getting a divorce.

They'd promise me Hawaii.
They'd promise me a horse,
If that made me not notice
They're getting a divorce.

The best will soon be coming,
And I know why, of course.
The worst's already happened:
They're getting a divorce.

Perfect

My dad made me pancakes for breakfast.
My mom said my haircut looked cool.
Instead of with grown-ups, they let me
Walk only with friends to my school.
My basketball got in the basket.
My history test got A-plus.
The backpack I lost was just found on
The trip-to-the-art-museum bus.
The allergy doctor is thinking
I might be okay with a cat.
The person I like a lot likes me.
(And that's all I'll say about that.)
Though nothing was GREAT or AMAZING,
Or even OH WOW or GEE WHIZ,
Today's what a perfect day feels like.
Today's what a perfect day is.

SONGS OF THE SEASONS

Shivery Winter Song

I'm freezing. I'm frozen. I'm froze.
From my head to the tips of my toes.
Both my right and left thumb
Are exceedingly numb
And I maybe am missing a nose.

I'm shaking. I'm shaken. I'm shook.
How I'd love to be reading a book
Somewhere cozy and nice.
Have my ears turned to ice?
Couldn't somebody please take a look?

I'm chilly. I'm chilling. I'm chilled.
If the winter were done, I'd be thrilled.
I keep thinking real hard
Of late June, our backyard,
And my dad making hamburgers—grilled.

But meanwhile I shiver and sting
From the biting winds Jan. and Feb. bring.
This is weather I hate.
So I'll just hibernate.
And don't bother to call me till spring.

Springtime

A Cautious Daffodil

Yesterday, some frost.
Tomorrow, maybe more frost.
Do I dare come out?

A Bird at the Bird Feeder

Somebody forgot
to put seed in my feeder.
Who's the birdbrain now?

A Lilac Bush Grows on the Shady Side of the Yard

Twisting and turning,
my eager purpled branches
stre............etch toward the light.

A Change

April's bashful buds
have gone all bright and brassy.
It's May, showing off.

A Writer Looks Out the Window

Everywhere every
thing's new. Got to write a few
new springtime haikus.

Stinky Summer Song

I'm so very glad that we've met.
But summertime sun makes me sweat,
And sweat makes me stinky
So I'll wave one pinky.
Back off—close you don't want to get.

If there's more that you wish me to tell,
Please stay far away and I'll yell.
But do not take a sniff,
Not the tiniest whiff.
You won't enjoy smelling my smell.

No book report, essay, or test.
Just shorts and a shirt, and you're dressed.
Sleeping late, running free.
If you don't inhale me,
The summer's the best of the best.

Autumn Leaves

Between the sizzle and the snow
The autumn leaves put on a show,
Twirling, whirling in the air,
Splashing color everywhere,
Making a commotion so
We won't forget them when they go.

Seasons

There's spring's soft greens,
Deep summer greens,
Then blazing golds and reds
In bold display beneath the autumn sun.
The dancing leaves retreat,
Become the crunch beneath our feet,
And then are done.

Their branches bared,
Their last leaves snared,
The shorn trees bow their heads,
As winter's forces gather to attack.
But while this planet spins,
What's gone returns, what ends begins,
And spring comes back.

MYSTERIES

Could Somebody Please Explain This to Me, Please?

Now there's a place for everything,
If you know where to look:
There's cupcakes in a bakery,
And stories in a book.

There's chicks and piglets on a farm,
And fishes in the seas.
There's cactuses in deserts, and
In forests, trees, trees, trees.

A sofa in the living room.
In night skies, the North Star.
You needn't be a wizard to
Discover where things are.

In pet shops, you'll find hamsters, and
In sports stores, balls and bats.
Department stores for boring stuff
Like scarves and gloves and hats.

There's mothers for a Band-Aid, and
There's iPods for a song.
So how come there's no place on Earth
Lost eyeglasses belong?

Mystery

Got sent to bed
Without dessert.
I hate to stare at ceilings.
But here I lie
Because I hurt
My little brother's feelings.
I cannot play
Computer games
Or watch TV at all,
Because I called
My brother names
You're not allowed to call.
Got sent to bed.
Got scolded, too.
Now here's the mystery:
How come the bad
Things that I do
Are always blamed on . . . me?

No Reason

For absolutely no reason at all my heart began to dance,
And something silvery sang inside my soul.
For absolutely no reason I was given another chance
To pick up the pieces and make what was broken whole.

For absolutely no reason I awoke this morning to learn
That I hadn't lost the race or failed the test.
What do you call a gift that you don't deserve and you didn't earn?
Call it blessed.

Toes

Except for ballerinas, whose
Poor toes are jammed in ballet shoes
So they can whirl and twirl upon
The stage, pretending they're a swan,
And not including all of those
In football or in soccer clothes,
Who need their toes to kick a ball and score,
I just can't figure out what toes are for.

Now fingers I can understand.
They're very handy on my hand
To hold my sandwich, scratch my head,
To draw a picture, make my bed,
To pick up stuff that I have dropped,
Or pick my nose (I've almost stopped),
Or help to carry bags home from the store.
But I can't figure out what toes are for.

I cannot kneel without a knee.
I need my eyes so I can see,
My ears to hear, my mouth to talk,
My legs and feet to take a walk.
And though I don't know what it means,
I'm told that all of us need spleens.
But I am finding it a hopeless chore
To try to figure out what toes are for.

Toes take up too much room in shoes,
But barefoot toes are quick to bruise.
And toenails grow so fast that they
Poke new holes in my socks each day.
I wish I had a pair of wings
Instead of these ten useless things
Impossible to like or to ignore.
Why can't I figure out what toes are for?

Snow White Talks to the Mirror

The magic mirror told the queen
She wasn't as pretty as I,
Which made the queen,
Who was jealous and mean,
Decide that I needed to die.

Mirror, mirror on the wall,
Why, I keep asking you, why
Didn't you lie?

Just Wondering

or

Something Else to Think About When You're Wide Awake in the Middle of the Night

I look at you. You look at me.
We're each a human being.
But how much of the person that
We're seeing are we seeing?

Is what you see when you see me
The me that I see too?
Is what I see when I see you
The you that's truly you?

Are we the same inside and out?
Or are there two of us:
The one that's shown. The one not known.
It's quite mysterious.

NOT DONE YET

Trying

I only cheated a tiny bit.
I never thought you'd notice it.
And besides, I wanted so badly to be the winner.
And it's true that I told a little white lie
When I said that I hadn't eaten the pie.
But I was starving, and it was forever till dinner.
This toy that I shouldn't have taken but did
Belonged, I admit, to a whole other kid.
But I'm hoping you won't think I'm a terrible sinner.
I know what I shouldn't. I know what I should.
And I'm trying my very best to be good.
I'm trying my very best—but I'm still a beginner.

Congrats!
01
01

Questions and Answers

What do you want to be when you're a grown-up?
That's what the teacher asked our class today.
The answers: talk-show host, spy, ballerina,
The president of the whole USA.
One girl's decided to become a rock star.
One boy is going for Olympic gold.
Two super-smart computer geeks expect to
Be zillionaires when they're nineteen years old.
Most everybody knew just what they wanted.
Most everybody seemed to have a plan:
A doctor, lawyer, teacher, movie-maker.
A chef, an astronaut, a fireman.
It looked like only I, and I alone,
Did not know what to be when I was grown.

Came home from school and snacked on milk and cookies.
Played with my friends Ricardo and Elyse.
Ric said when he grew up he'd be a writer.
El said when she grew up she'd make world peace.
We watched cartoons, did stuff on my mom's laptop,
Rode bikes, then tossed the ball around out back.
Went in my room and finished up a puzzle.
Went in the kitchen for another snack.
Tonight I thought again about that question.
Decided I liked everything I did.
And so, instead of answering, I'm asking,
When I grow up, could I still be a kid?

Manners

Burping's rude and slurping's rude
And talking with your mouth full's rude.
So's leaving out your "thank you" and your "please."
Interrupting people? Rude!
Texting during dinner? Rude!
So's using sleeves, not tissues, when you sneeze.

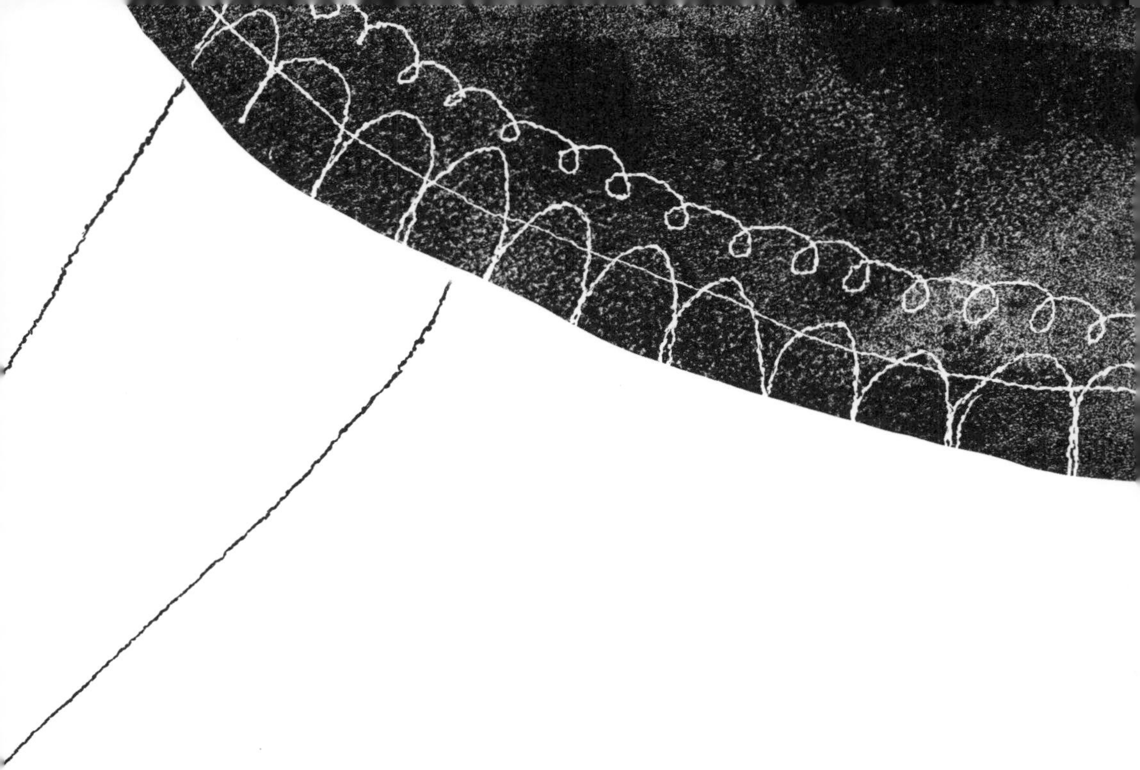

Bragging's rude and cursing's rude.
Both loud and silent farting's rude.
So's going next when next is not your turn.
Whatever's feeling right to do
Is never what's polite to do.
And that's what's making manners hard to learn.

In Between

Too old to need a night-light and
Too young to drive a car.
Too young for *War and Peace*, too old
For *Where the Wild Things Are.*
Too young to drink a latte and
Too old for sippy cups.
I'm in between and sometimes
I can't tell the downs from ups.

Too old to cry at flu shots and
Too young for a tattoo.
Too young for movies rated R,
Too old for Scooby-Doo.
Too old for booster seats, too young
For my own credit card.
I'm in between and often
In between is very hard.

Too young to give up whining and
Too old to run amok.
Too young for Don Giovanni and
Too old for Donald Duck.
Too old to keep my teddy bear,
Too young to let him go.
I'm in between and waiting
For the rest of me to grow.